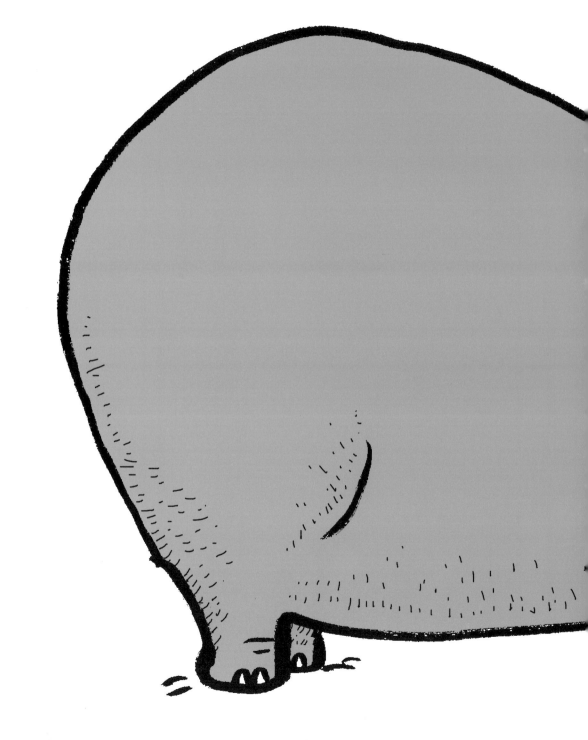

Patricia von Pleasantsquirrel

by James Proimos

Dial Books for Young Readers

For Jolie
Love, James

DIAL BOOKS FOR YOUNG READERS
A division of Penguin Young Readers Group
Published by The Penguin Group
Penguin Group (USA) Inc., 375 Hudson Street, New York, NY 10014, U.S.A.
Penguin Group (Canada), 90 Eglinton Avenue East, Suite 700, Toronto, Ontario, Canada M4P 2Y3 (a division of Pearson Penguin Canada Inc.)
Penguin Books Ltd, 80 Strand, London WC2R 0RL, England
Penguin Ireland, 25 St. Stephen's Green, Dublin 2, Ireland (a division of Penguin Books Ltd)
Penguin Group (Australia), 250 Camberwell Road, Camberwell, Victoria 3124, Australia (a division of Pearson Australia Group Pty Ltd)
Penguin Books India Pvt Ltd, 11 Community Centre, Panchsheel Park, New Delhi - 110 017, India
Penguin Group (NZ), 67 Apollo Drive, Rosedale, North Shore, New Zealand (a division of Pearson New Zealand Ltd)
Penguin Books (South Africa) (Pty) Ltd, 24 Sturdee Avenue, Rosebank, Johannesburg 2196, South Africa
Penguin Books Ltd, Registered Offices: 80 Strand, London WC2R 0RL, England

Designed by Jasmin Rubero
Text set in Catseye
Manufactured in China on acid-free paper

1 3 5 7 9 10 8 6 4 2

Library of Congress Cataloging-in-Publication Data
available upon request

ONCE there was a princess
who had not yet found her princessdom.

Her name was
Patricia von Pleasantsquirrel.

You may curtsy.

Patricia's mother said she could not stay up until midnight.

Her father forbade her from having cake before dinner.

Her baby brother acted fussy when he should have been acting as her personal servant.

WAAaaH!

Patricia's dog was not a great white stallion.
He was just a dog.

Arf.

Patricia was certain that a one-level, three-bedroom, moatless cottage was no place for royalty.

That night Patricia wore her frilliest dress

Frilly

and took out one book after another

and settled on one.

Where the Wild Things Are

Hmmm.

And thought this:

If a silly boy with no social graces could be made king with no effort at all, then imagine how easy it would be for me to find my princessdom.

She immediately packed her cardboard crown,

her collection of Wedgwood china,

and her two favorite jelly beans.

Edith Wharton

Louisa May Alcott

She said good-bye to her fish. Her fish understood her.

She got in her airplane

and flew

and flew

AND FLEW

FAR AWAY.

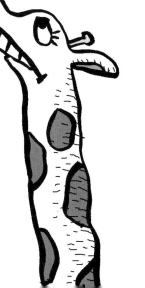

Finally, Patricia von Pleasantsquirrel
arrived in the Land of the Hippos.

"Please bring me to the top hippo," she said.

The flashiest hippo stepped forward. His name was Elvis.

"May I be your princess?"

"I don't see why not," said Elvis.

The hippos had a big party to celebrate Patricia

being named their princess.

At the party Patricia met Cynthia.

Cynthia was the former princess.

"Thank you, thank you, thank you for taking my job as princess," said Cynthia.

"No problemo," said Patricia.

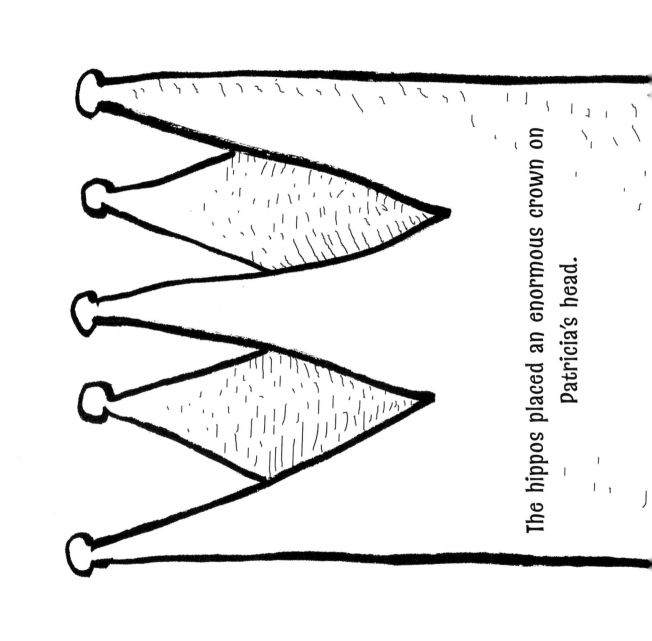

The hippos placed an enormous crown on Patricia's head.

It was not made of cardboard.

They fed Patricia cake before dinner
and more cake FOR dinner

and even more cake for dessert.

They danced all night,   past midnight,

and in and out of the next day.

Patricia was given a great white stallion.

She rode him for three straight days.

On the fourth day Patricia was handed a list
of her princessly duties.

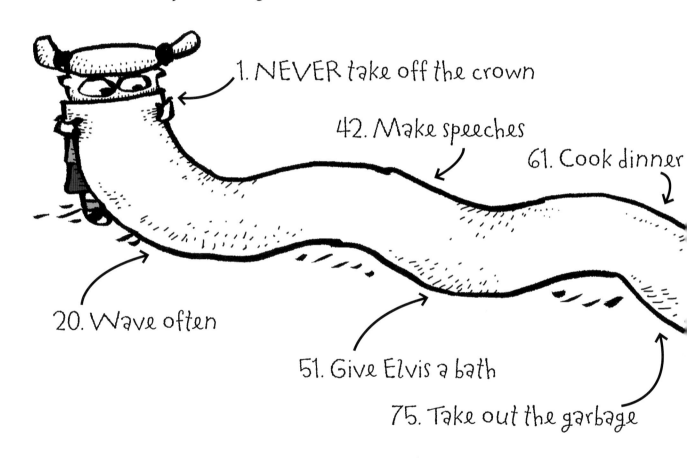

1. NEVER take off the crown

42. Make speeches

61. Cook dinner

20. Wave often

51. Give Elvis a bath

75. Take out the garbage

98. Read EVERYONE
a bedtime story

230. Get up at five
in the morning and
crow like a rooster

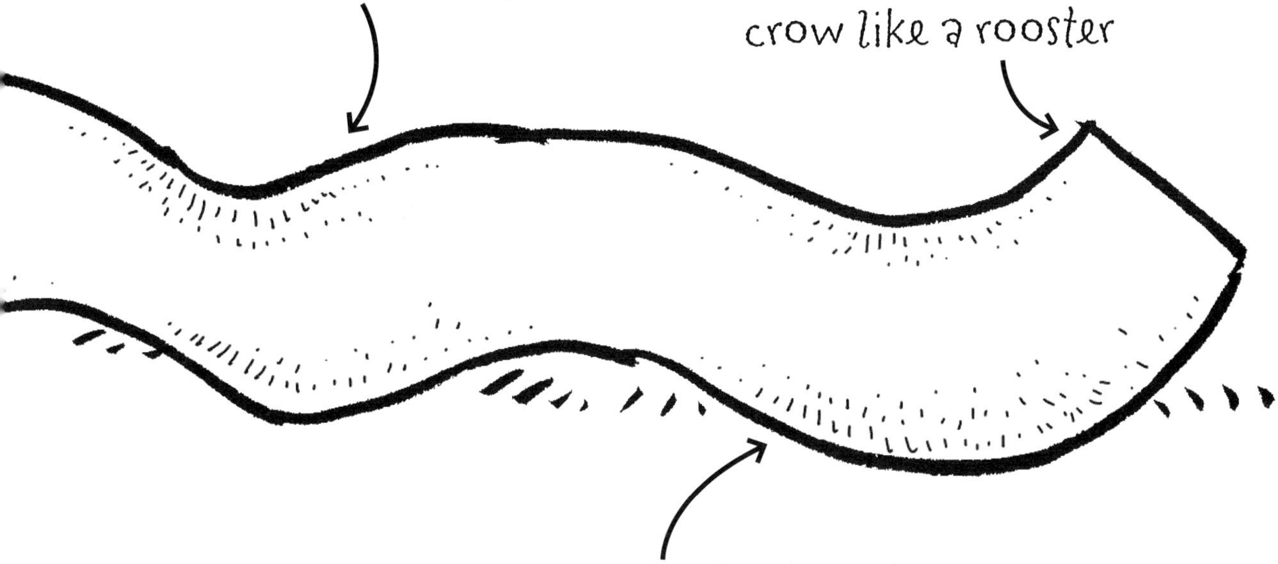

120. Tuck EVERYONE in

For what felt like weeks, Patricia
never took off the crown,
waved often,
made speeches,
gave Elvis a bath,

took out the garbage,
cooked dinner,
read everyone a bedtime story,
tucked them all in,

and got up at five every morning to
crow like a rooster.

DOODLE doodle doo!

But the crown
was getting very heavy.
Very heavy indeed.

One day Patricia took the crown off.

You took off the crown!
Now you must go!"

shouted the hippos.

"But—"

"Now!"

Patricia was stunned.
But there was nothing she could do.

Before she left
she said good-bye to Cynthia.
Cynthia understood her.

PATRICIA FLEW

and flew

Y'all go on, now!

AND FLEW.

Vous allez Fille.

沒有地方像家

When Patricia arrived home,
her mother didn't permit her to
stay up until midnight.

Her father did not allow her to
have cake before dinner.

She was not waited on by her little brother.

And her dog was still just a dog.

A wonderful, beautiful, incredible dog.

That night she put on a big old T-shirt that her parents had bought for her.

She hadn't worn it for a long time.

Patricia took out one book after another

and finally settled on one.

She read it to the fish.

The Giving Tree

After a long discussion they decided they had no idea what it was really about.

And they went to bed
happier than two princesses
could ever be.

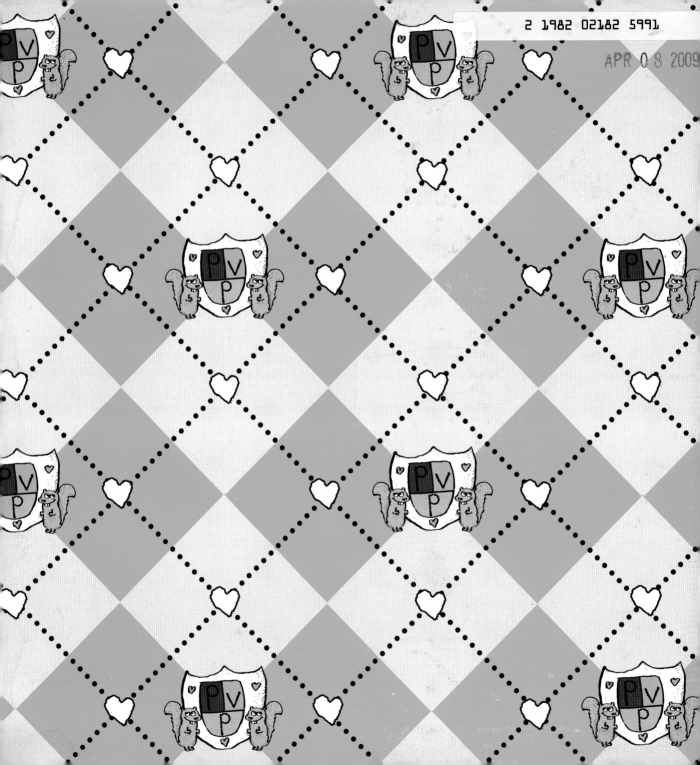